ALSO BY JEFFREY MOUSSAIEFF MASSON

Slipping into Paradise: Why I Live in New Zealand

The Pig Who Sang to the Moon: The Emotional World of Farm Animals

The Nine Emotional Lives of Cats: A Journey into the Feline Heart

The Evolution of Fatherhood: A Celebration of Animal and Human Families

Dogs Never Lie About Love:
Reflections on the Emotional World of Dogs

The Wild Child: The Unsolved Mystery of Kaspar Hauser

When Elephants Weep:
The Emotional Lives of Animals (with Susan McCarthy)

My Father's Guru:
A Journey Through Spirituality and Disillusion

Final Analysis: The Making and Unmaking of a Psychoanalyst

Against Therapy: Emotional Tyranny and the Myth of Psychological Healing

A Dark Science: Women, Sexuality, and Psychiatry in the Nineteenth Century

The Assault on Truth: Freud's Suppression of the Seduction Theory

The Oceanic Feeling:
The Origins of Religious Sentiment in Ancient India

The Complete Letters of Sigmund Freud
to Wilhelm Fliess 1887–1904 (editor)

The Peacock's Egg: Love Poems from Ancient India
(editor, translations by W. S. Merwin)

The Dhvanyaloka of Anandavardhana with the Locana of Abhinavagupta
(translator, with D. H. H. Ingalls and M. V. Patwardhan)

Love's Enchanted World: The Avimaraka (with D. D. Kosambi)

The Rasadhyaya of the Natyasastra
(translator and editor, with M. V. Patwardhan; two volumes)

Santarasa and Abhinvagupta's Philosophy of Aesthetics

Dogs Have the Strangest Friends,
and Other True Stories of Animal Feelings (for children)

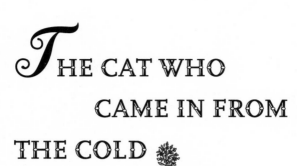

THE CAT WHO CAME IN FROM THE COLD

THE CAT WHO CAME IN FROM THE COLD

A Fable

JEFFREY MOUSSAIEFF MASSON

Ballantine Books
New York

A Ballantine Book
Published by The Random House Publishing Group

www.ballantinebooks.com

Library of Congress Cataloging-in-Publication Data:
Masson, J. Moussaieff (Jeffrey Moussaieff), 1941–
The cat who came in from the cold : a fable /
Jeffrey Moussaieff Masson.—1st ed.
p.   cm.
ISBN 0-345-47866-5—ISBN 0-345-47867-3 (tr.)
1. Cats—Fiction. 2. India—Fiction. 3. Human-animal
relationships—Fiction. I. Title.

PR9639.4.M35C37 2004

823'.914—dc22   2004051908

Manufactured in the United States of America

First Edition: November 2004

2 4 6 8 9 7 5 3 1

Design by Mercedes Everett

To Nancy Miller,
my editor for twenty years

Acknowledgments

I want to thank Christiane Bird for helping me turn three different versions of this story into a readable whole. She did a magnificent job, and without her, this book would not be at all.

Thanks to Robert Goldman, professor of Sanskrit at the University of California at Berkeley, for providing texts and helpful consultation.

Finally, thanks to the many felines who have shared my home over the last sixty-three years and agreed to teach me the wisdom and beauty of the way of the cat.

Author's Note

I have always been intrigued by what could possibly have induced the cat—that divinely aloof and independent creature—to choose to live among humans. I use the word *choose* deliberately; anyone familiar with feline ways will know that while we may have welcomed that first feline friend with open arms, it surely was the cat who chose us. Cats can't really be coerced to do anything, of course; much of the time they seem merely to tolerate us, although when they like, their affection can bind them to us as one.

It was in this spirit of inquiry that I set out to tell the story of Billi, an Asian leopard cat in ancient India. Drawing on the wisdom of Sanskrit texts I had studied long ago, and knowledge I have gained in recent years about the complex world of animal emotions, I have attempted to pinpoint the moment when the first cat made the choice of domestication, a moment that has opened both our species to a relationship that for thousands of years has provided mutual fulfillment, love, and respect—at least on our part—across the species barrier.

THE CAT WHO
CAME IN FROM
THE COLD

Thousands of years ago, in the forests of south India, Billi sat on his favorite branch of his favorite mango tree in his favorite mango orchard, admiring himself. He stretched out one fine paw, then another. He washed his face. He flicked his tail. He examined his black and brown spots. How strong, how handsome, how glorious, to be an Asian leopard cat!

A cloud passed before the sun, and Billi inched forward on his branch, the better to bask in the fading rays. He loved being so small and light. His huge cousins the lions and tigers, for all their strength and might, could never stretch out on a limb as slim as this. Or slip so easily through the forest shrub. Or pass unnoticed in and out of human villages at night. Billi closed his eyes in contentment. He dozed, dreaming of a fat, squeaking mouse trapped between his paws as he batted it back and forth. He would go hunting later, after the sun went down.

"Hurry up, Nandini, Mother is waiting."

Billi opened one eye. Small two-foots were approaching. He peered down through the leaves, at bright flashes of red and yellow. Below walked a boy child and a girl child, their black hair shining, their thin arms and legs swinging. Billi liked to see small humans. Their high voices reminded him of springtime, their faces reminded him of the moon. Too bad they grew up to be adults.

"It's not my fault, it's Janaka," the girl child said. "He's still back by the river."

"Janaka!" the boy child shouted, and a few moments later, a big brown dog bounded up. Barking excitedly, he ran circles around the children, as if he hadn't seen them for days instead of minutes, and slathered them with dog kisses.

Billi turned his face away in disgust. What was the matter with dogs? He didn't have anything against canines per se, but the way they showered affection on their two-footed friends was ridiculous. Even worse was the way dogs had relinquished their freedom to be safely housed and fed by humans. Where was their dignity? Where was their pride? How could they give up something as priceless as independence for something as mundane as security?

Another, darker cloud passed before the sun, and Billi shivered. It was almost October. The monsoons would be here soon.

"Only five more days until Diwali," the girl child said, as if reading his thoughts. The monsoons and Diwali, the biggest human festival of the year, always came together. "Mother has already started cooking. . . ."

"Talib's uncles and aunts are arriving tomorrow. . . ."

The children's voices faded away as they disappeared in the direction of their village. Billi started down from his branch. The dark clouds were rolling in now, packing the sky, and the sunshine was gone. His good mood had disappeared. He dreaded the start of the monsoon season, when huge storm clouds darkened the sky for days on end until it felt as if something terrible, something irrevocable, were about to happen. And then, when the lightning started to flash and the thunder to roar— It was like a preamble to the end of all living things, to the whole world coming apart.

Missing his footing, Billi was astonished to find himself suddenly falling. What in the name of Krishna—? he wondered as the world rushed past. How had he miscalculated his step so badly? He twisted his body and stretched out his front legs just in time to land on them gracefully, arching his back to absorb the shock. Landing safely from a fall was child's play, really—he couldn't understand why so many other animals got so badly hurt, even after a short fall from a low branch.

Still, it was embarrassing—a grown cat falling for no good reason. Surreptitiously Billi looked around, to see if anyone had been watching, and started licking his paws and grooming his pelt, feigning nonchalance, just in case—

"I saw that."

Billi stiffened. Who said that?

"You fell off the tree." The big brown dog was back.

"I did not," Billi said.

The dog just grinned, wagging his tail, and Billi continued passing his paws over his face and chest, determined to hide his embarrassment by cleaning off a few specks of dust.

"How can you be such a fool about humans?" he asked the dog when he was finished.

The dog was now rolling around in the dirt, his long pink tongue hanging out. "What do you mean?" he said. "They're my friends. We have fun together."

"But you're their slave."

"Says who?" the dog said. "I think it's the other way around. They feed me and play with me and take me for walks. All I have to do is be happy and wag my tail."

A whistle came from the village and the dog sat up. "Gotta go in a minute," he said.

"See what I mean?" Billi said.

"Well, it's a lot

more fun hanging out with them than it is with you," the dog said. "You apparently only want to be by yourself."

"And what's wrong with that?"

But Billi was talking to the air. The dog had already run off. What an idiot! Billi thought. He obviously knows nothing about cats. It's true that I like being alone—we cats relish our independence, but we also like to play and to explore and to watch. We're curious about everything that moves and everything that doesn't. We smell every flower, watch every butterfly, examine every tree. We chase after shadows and insects just for the joy of running, and bat sticks and nuts around just for the pleasure of play. I know and appreciate this forest thoroughly—much better than that crude dog.

Haughtily, Billi raised his tail straight in the air and padded down the path toward his evening hunting grounds and home cave. Twilight was descending, and the night sounds and smells of the forest were beginning. The calls of the parrots, the chattering of the monkeys, the croaking of the frogs. The perfume of the breezes, the moisture of the mists, the musk of the loam beneath his paws. All was right in the world. He lived in paradise.

Billi wished at that moment, resting on the soft dirt floor of his cave, that he could share his contentment with someone—he had an almost unbearable urge to purr—but here was the problem, here, perhaps—just perhaps—the dog was right. . . . Cats not only liked to be alone, they *had* to be alone, it was part of their nature, and this meant that there was never anyone around to purr to or to talk to. No cat that Billi knew of lived among other cats, let alone other animals, except in early childhood. Why was that? he wondered. And was that really a good situation? Being a slave to the twofoots was one thing, but having another animal around to talk to and play with now and again . . . surely that was something else.

Billi thought back to his childhood. Like most cats, he had never known his father and had barely known his mother and siblings. After all, they'd lived together for only six short months, during which time his mother was often out hunting, leaving Billi and his sisters and brothers alone for hours on end. They'd all played tag together—he felt happy, remembering that—and rolled over and over one another in the tall grasses surrounding their cave. He could still picture his biggest sister's bright black eyes and his smallest brother's scrawny, crooked tail. But that was all. Their time together had been so short. He'd never seen any of his brothers and sisters as adults. For all he knew, they could be dead.

He could remember his mother only a bit better. Her kind, broad face. Her long, ticklish whiskers. The occasional cuff of her then seemingly gigantic paw when he'd tumbled against her just a little too hard. She was a handsome feline, too, of that he was certain. He'd inherited her good looks.

Billi remembered one day when his mother returned to their cave a little later than usual, a little more tired than usual. His siblings were all asleep when she came in, but he was wide awake and waiting. An odd, skinny, two-footed creature had passed within ten yards of the cave that day, and Billi had a million questions—

"They're called humans, or two-foots," his mother said. "And they're very different from us. They don't like being alone. They live together in families all their lives. When many families live together, it's called a village. And when many, many families live together, it's called a city."

Then she told Billi a strange story that had haunted him all his life.

"Many years ago, long before you were born, a horrible thing happened to me," she said. "I was out hunting in the tall grasses near the river one evening when I thought I saw a strange shape just ahead of me. But before I could stop myself, I took another step and heard something crashing behind me. It was a door! I had stepped into a trap! I was terrified. I howled for hours and hours. I knew the trap had been set by humans, and I was sure they would kill me. Humans love our fur! They make it into rugs and coats. But that's not what happened. A ratty little man came the next morning, shoved me into a dirty white bag, and took me to a market where I was sold as an exotic pet."

"A pet!" Billi said, horrified, even though he wasn't sure exactly what the word meant.

"Yes, or at least that's what the humans thought. But I would never be their pet. Never, never! To be docile and treated like a dog? Impossible! I fought tooth and nail every time anyone approached me. I hissed and scratched, I spat and howled. The people who bought me were terrified. They kept me in a small cage and never let me out."

"You must have been miserable," Billi said. He snuggled closer to his mother. To think that such an abominable thing had happened to her!

"Yes, I was," she said. "But it did give me the chance to observe two-foots firsthand, which I found to be quite interesting. They wanted me as a pet not because they liked me and wanted to be my friend, but because I was a status symbol. I made them feel important. Neighbors were impressed by how good-looking and 'wild' I was."

"What's a status symbol?" Billi asked.

"It's something good that one human has that other humans want but can't afford, which makes them jealous. Humans like to make other humans jealous. A status symbol is usually very expensive, and it's not a living creature—it's a thing. Those two-foots never showed me any respect, and they certainly never tried to make me happy."

"Did that make you hate humans?"

"Yes and no. You see, there was a small boy living in the house, maybe five or six years old. He was very gentle with me—not like the others. He would come and sit by my cage for hours, talking to me, saying kind things. I loved the sound of his voice, and sometimes I purred for him. Only for him. He never told anyone. It was our secret. In a way, we were friends."

"What did his parents say?" Billi asked. "Didn't they notice?"

"No, they paid as little attention to him as they did to me. They were not a nice family."

"How did you escape?"

"The boy felt sorry for me, and one afternoon when everyone else was asleep, he let me go. He looked frightened when he opened my cage. Not because of me—he knew I wouldn't hurt him—but because of his father. That boy saved my life. I would have died if I'd stayed in that cage. After the boy let me out, I walked over to him and licked his hand. I was so grateful!"

"What did he do?"

"He cried. He wanted me to stay. But I

couldn't, of course. I ran out the door, through the garden, and into the forest. I never saw him again." Billi's mother paused, wrinkling her whiskers. "But the funny thing is, I can't seem to get the image of that little boy crying out of my mind. I remember it every day. It's as if there's some unfinished business there. But I can't imagine what it could be."

"I'd like to have a human friend," Billi said.

"Don't talk nonsense."

"No, really, I would."

"Hush, now. Go to sleep. Cats don't have human friends."

Billi curled up more closely against his mother, listening to her heart and to the hearts of his nearest siblings. He knew his mother was right. But why?

The next morning when Billi awoke, his mother was gone. That wasn't unusual, but that evening, she didn't come home. He never saw her again. Three days later, two of Billi's siblings disappeared, and the day after that two more. For the next five days, only Billi and his youngest sister were left, and then, suddenly, she was gone, too. Billi was alone. He moped around the empty cave, continually sniffing the hollow in which his mother had once lain, trying not to make embarrassing mewing sounds. He knew that this was the way it had to be—mother cats always deserted their kittens when they were old enough to live on their own, and siblings never stayed together. But still, he couldn't help but wish, How lovely it would be . . . if only things were different—

Billi shook himself hard, back into the present. What was wrong with him? He was an adult now and shouldn't be thinking about such childish things. Or about the past. Cats never thought about the past— living fully and gloriously in the present was one of the greatest things about his species. He must have been thrown off balance by that rude dog, and that ridiculous fall, and the depressing hint of the impending monsoons. . . . Billi always got a funny feeling with the coming of the monsoons. He wasn't sure where it came from or what it meant. Sometimes it seemed to be a nostalgia, a longing, a wistfulness, a regret for something he missed, but what could that be? How could he miss something he'd never known?

The next afternoon, Billi was back on his favorite branch of his favorite mango tree in his favorite mango orchard. The morning had been overcast, but now the sun was shining. With any luck, the monsoons were still a few days away.

Billi yawned and daydreamed, stretched and basked in the sun. But every time he slipped off into a catnap, something immediately woke him up. The orchard abutted a path leading to small villages in one direction, the river and other villages in the other. Billi always had much to see from his perch—one of its great advantages. But today, there was almost *too* much to see. The human foot traffic never seemed to stop. Everyone was coming and going, in preparation for the festival of Diwali.

Billi watched with interest. Diwali had nothing to do with him, of course—cats never celebrated anything—but he loved it anyway. He loved seeing travelers hurrying along the path, journeying long distances just to be with their families for the holidays. He loved seeing the humans' many strange bundles and packages, some filled with food, some with fine clothes, some with toys for the children. He loved watching the laying in of provisions—piles and piles of firewood, rice, lentils, spices, and nuts. The provisions had to last not only through the five days of the festival, but also through the long, dreary monsoon season that followed. Humans rarely left their homes during the monsoon season. Instead, they holed up with the tools of their trade—scholars with their manuscripts, farmers with their farm implements, fishermen with their boats and nets—and spent three months reading, studying, fixing, mending, and cleaning indoors. And at night, as the torrential rains continually poured, the humans gathered in boisterous groups to play games, sing songs, dance dances, and tell stories.

Sometimes, after the Diwali festival started but before the monsoon rains began, Billi would slip down into the villages at night, to watch and smell the festive goings-on—lights and music, singing and dancing, fried stuffed breads, curries made with ghee. How he envied the two-foots then. He usually spent most of Diwali and all of the monsoon season alone in his cave, venturing out only when the rains abated momentarily to catch himself some lunch or dinner.

Billi never ventured into the village during the day because there was no telling how humans would react. He was only a small cat—not much bigger than a rooster, really—but he was "wild," and many people panicked at the sight of him. Sometimes they even tried to kill him. What fools these humans could be.

"Come on, Nandini, hurry up!"

Billi peered down from his perch. The same boy child and girl child he'd seen the day before were approaching. They were carrying large bundles of firewood, and the girl child, Nandini, was staggering under its weight, as if she might collapse at any minute. Billi blinked to himself. She was funny.

"Out of the way, children, out of the way." Five or six adults loaded with bundles were bustling past. What's in those bags? Billi wondered, craning his neck to see until the entourage passed out of sight.

"Where's Janaka?" Nandini said. She had stopped walking and was swaying to and fro under her load.

"I don't know," the boy child said. "But don't worry about him now. He'll catch up."

"Oh, look!" Nandini dropped her firewood and clapped her hands. "Here he comes. He's helping us!"

The big brown dog galloped up, carrying a large stick in his mouth.

"Good dog, good dog! You're so smart!" Nandini said, and threw her arms around the dog's neck. He dropped his stick and began licking her face. She kissed his nose. Then the boy child dropped his bundle, too, and the three of them began chasing one another around and around the mango orchard. The children were shouting and laughing, the dog was barking and pretending to growl. Reaching a far corner of the orchard, he bent low on his front paws, daring the children to come closer, and when they did, he charged off again, wagging his tail.

"What's so smart about carrying a stick?" Billi grumbled to himself. But he couldn't help watching the children and dog. They did look as though they were having fun.

Then, as suddenly as it had started, it was over. Panting, the children picked up their bundles of firewood and started for home, followed by the dog, who, Billi noticed, was no longer carrying his stick. So much for his so-called smarts. Dogs had nothing over cats.

"I can see you, you know."

Billi froze. The dog was back.

"You're up there on that skinny branch, pretending to be invisible."

Billi didn't say a word. Why should he?

"Why don't you come down and play?"

Billi yawned.

"Come on." The dog danced forward a few steps, challenging him, then danced back. "Or why not chase me from up there? You run on the branches, I'll run on the ground. Come on, it'll be fun."

Billi hesitated. It did sound like fun. But since when did cats play with dogs?

"Janaka!" the boy child was calling.

"Too late," the dog said, and bounded off.

Alone again, Billi felt relieved. Or did he? He wouldn't have minded a short romp with the dog. A very short romp, that is.

If nothing else, he should have thought to ask the dog, who seemed the type to know everyone, about the Sanskrit scholar. Billi hadn't seen the old man in

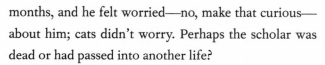

months, and he felt worried—no, make that curious—about him; cats didn't worry. Perhaps the scholar was dead or had passed into another life?

The Sanskrit scholar had been the very first human Billi had ever observed close up. Back then, Billi was still new to his orchard and had yet to discover his favorite branch. Instead, he was sitting on a bigger branch of an older tree, a little farther from the river, and had just settled down for a snooze when he saw the old man approaching. He had three vertical white lines painted on his forehead, and his head was shaved, with a tiny gray ponytail in back. A long cotton cloth passed between his legs, and in his hands was a well-thumbed manuscript.

The old man had headed to Billi's now favorite tree and took a seat at its base. Hypnotically, he began to chant something that sounded like poetry, but Billi couldn't understand a word. Whatever the deep, mysterious, musical language was, it wasn't anything like Malayalam, the languages people spoke in the villages. A few minutes later, half a dozen boys, also dressed in long cotton cloths, joined the old man, settling down into a circle around him. This was a school, Billi realized suddenly. The man was a teacher. He was teaching the boys Sanskrit, the ancient language of India. Intrigued, Billi crept closer and listened hard.

Billi had always loved languages, ever since he was a kitten. He had learned Malayalam by prowling around the villages at night, listening beneath people's windows, and could speak and understand all the languages of the other animals in the forest. Sanskrit was an especially difficult language, Billi knew, but he felt hooked by its hypnotic cadence and couldn't resist coming back to the class the next morning. And the morning after that. And the morning after that. Soon he began picking up a word here, a word there, and started speaking Sanskrit to himself at night. It wasn't as if there were anyone in his life to distract him from his studies. In fact, if the scholar only knew it, Billi was his most diligent student, never missing a class and the chance to listen to the classical Sanskrit texts. Patanjali's *Yoga Sutras.* The *Mahabharata.* The Upanishads. The *Ramayana.*

One day, Billi was startled to hear the scholar speak his name—"Billi." He crouched, tensed and ready to flee if necessary. Had the old man or the boys discovered him?

There it was again, "Billi." But no one was looking up at the tree. He listened hard and heard the scholar say that *billi*, the Hindi word for "cat"—Billi already knew that—came from the Sanskrit word *vidalah*. And that the *vidalah* figured prominently in two classical Sanskrit texts.

Well, what do you know, Billi thought. Maybe humans thought more about cats than he'd realized. From what he'd observed, humans were an extraordinarily self-absorbed race, with little interest in any species but their own.

The scholar then began reading a passage from a fable from Purnabhadra's *Pancatantra*. It was a fable about an argument between a partridge and a hare. Each claimed to be the owner of the same hole under a tree, and they decided to find an impartial judge to settle the matter. "The partridge said to the hare: 'But who will look into our lawsuit?' The hare said: 'Why, here is this aged cat named White-ears, who lives on the bank of the river, practicing penance, and who feels compassion for all sentient beings. He knows the sacred law; he will make the right decision for us.'

"The partridge answered: 'Leave that mean creature

be!' For has it not been said: 'Do not trust one who disguises himself with the mask of an ascetic.' "

But since they had no one else to turn to, the two animals made their way down to the river, where they found "White-ears, who had taken on a false self in order to make an easy living without having to work. In order to win their confidence, he stood up on two legs and gazed without blinking at the sun, and with outstretched arms, one eye closed, he began to pray. As he prayed their hearts opened up to him in trust, and they came closer, and told him about their dispute over the dwelling: 'O ascetic, teacher of the law, we have a dispute; so decide it for us according to the law codes!'

"White-ears replied, 'I have become old and my senses are no longer so acute such that I cannot hear very well from a distance. Come up very close to me and speak loudly.' They came closer to him and told him their story. Then White-ears, winning their confidence so as to make them come even closer, recited texts from the law books:

" 'When righteousness is destroyed, it destroys in turn; when righteousness is preserved, it preserves.

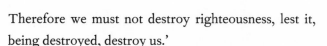

Therefore we must not destroy righteousness, lest it, being destroyed, destroy us.'

"To make a long story short, by such hypocrisy he was able to win their confidence to such an extent that they came right up to his lap; and then with one blow from his paw they were both caught and killed by that evil creature."

What a slanderous story, Billi thought, horrified, as the scholar's words trailed off. Is this what men think of cats? How ill informed they are! Cats are never hypocritical—that's one of the reasons we prefer to remain independent. We would rather walk alone than pretend to be something we are not or to believe something we do not.

Billi was so angry that he considered never returning to Sanskrit class. But after only a one-day boycott, his curiosity got the better of him. What was the other classical Sanskrit text that mentioned cats? And what else might he learn from the scholar? The old man was very wise. After reading the *Pancatantra* story, he spoke for a long time about the dangers of religious hypocrisy and the importance of being true to oneself. Billi pondered both subjects for some time. Cats weren't religious, and he couldn't imagine ever being a believer, but he could see the appeal of south India's three major religions—Buddhism, Hinduism, and Jainism—or at least, the appeal of their ideals. He especially liked the religions' shared belief in harming no living being, animal or human—the doctrine of ahimsa.

As for being true to oneself, well, wasn't that exactly the issue that Billi was constantly grappling with? Who was his true self? A solitary creature who lived and hunted entirely alone, coupling only with females for short periods now and again? That certainly was *supposed* to be his nature. He was a cat. But why did he have these strange, noncatlike yearnings to be with other creatures, especially humans, to have a friend?

Every now and again, during the long and studious mornings, Billi suspected that the scholar was aware of his presence. He had a way of glancing up toward Billi's branch when he arrived and of staring skyward after he had finished a particularly moving passage. He never looked at Billi directly, but Billi liked imagining that the two of them shared a secret—the secret of his presence—linking them together.

One day the scholar told his students of a trip he'd taken to the Coromandel Coast, on the Bay of Bengal. There, he'd come across Mahabalipuram, a famous temple complex that contained the world's largest bas-relief, depicting the descent from heaven to earth of the celestial Ganges River. As the story went, the god Shiva, alarmed that the river's descending torrent might drown the world, allowed the flood to trickle through his matted hair. Every creature on earth emerged from the forest to watch. Among them was the elephant, carved in his real size, and the so-called Cat Who Wanted to Be an Ascetic. The relief showed the cat standing on one foot on the banks of the Ganges, doing rigorous penance, eyes firmly shut, fasting, praying, immobile, and seemingly paying no attention to the rats and mice that had come from all over to pay homage to him. Billi shivered at the image and wondered at the mysterious connection between animals and two-foots.

Many months later, the scholar finally read the second classical Sanskrit text about cats. But to Billi's extreme disappointment, the *Mahabharata* basically told the same story as the *Pancatantra*, and in even more incendiary language: O King, once upon a time, an evil cat stationed himself on the banks of the Ganges, and kept one arm raised to the heavens as penance, pretending to have purified his heart of all malice to any creature. After a long time had gone by, all animals born of an egg began to trust him, and approaching him all together, they praised that cat. Worshiped by all birds, this eater of birds knew he had what he wanted. After an even greater time, mice went to that place. And these also were convinced he was a person of virtue, who took vows of penance. And having decided that he [was to be trusted], they determined the following: We have many enemies. This pious cat should act as our maternal uncle, and protect those of us who are very young and those of us who are very old. Then that mean cat whose soul was filled with evil, feeding on mice, gradually got fat and his complexion was good, and he became strong in his limbs. All the mice then, quickly took counsel of one another: The cat grows, and we diminish. Then a very old and wise mouse, by the name of Kolika, said these just words: "Our uncle does not really want to be an ascetic. He is a hypocrite,

and has pretended to be our friend when in reality he is
our enemy."

Curses! Billi was so furious, even now, three months
later, remembering the passage, that he almost fell out of
the tree. What was wrong with these humans! Had anyone ever bothered consulting a cat about that story?
Why did two-foots have so many misconceptions about
cats? They should take a good look at their own behavior
sometime instead of condemning the behavior of others.

Selfish and self-involved, Billi growled, they call us
selfish and self-involved? What about wealthy humans?
Ambitious humans? Happy humans? How often do
they notice their less fortunate cousins?

Sadists, they call us sadists, he fumed—just because
we play with mice before we kill them? Pure slander!
We're practicing our skills and giving the mice a sport-
ing chance. The end is swift and painless. We take no
pleasure in their suffering. Or kill for the sake of killing.
Can humans make the same claim?

Envious, they think us envious? Never have I
known a cat who envied the life of another. We're jealous sometimes, maybe, but never anything as sinister
and self-defeating as envious.

Of limited intelligence, they claim—us? Stupid? Humans are the ones who are always comparing their intelligence to other two-foots and to other species. *That's* what's stupid. Every being is intelligent in its own way.

Smug? *We're* smug?

Billi spent the first day of Diwali studiously avoiding humans. He'd been thinking about them far too much lately. It was time for him to reaffirm his independent ways and go birding and fishing in the mangroves.

Billi lived on the edge of the coastal Kerala backwaters, famed throughout south India for its vast network of lagoons, lakes, rivers, and canals, along which grew great tropical trees with thick prop roots. The mangroves were home to dozens of species of birds—teals, gulls, cormorants, grebes, herons, egrets, spoonbills— that Billi liked to hunt, creeping through the grasses, his back low and flat, barely making a sound. But the birds were smart, and quick! For every one that he caught, dozens escaped. Not that he cared too much. Eating was only half the fun. Just as exciting was the chase itself—

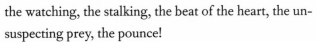

the watching, the stalking, the beat of the heart, the un-suspecting prey, the pounce!

The mangroves were also home to the tasty karimeen fish, one of Billi's favorite foods. He could spend hours sitting by a river, waiting for the telltale flash of silver. And as soon as he saw it, in went his paw, down into the cold and wet. He had to remember to watch his back for crocodiles, though; it was easy to become oblivious, waiting for a fish.

Humans cruised the shallow Kerala backwaters in small passenger boats that they pushed along with bamboo poles or in bigger work boats that they used to transport dried coconut meat, cashews, and other goods. Billi liked to watch the vessels as they passed and, when near the more open lakes, kept an eye out for the sailing boats that sometimes floated in the distance.

On that first day of Diwali, Billi was in luck. He had an exciting near miss with a tasty-looking grebe, followed by a fast-paced chase after an injured teal, who flew from branch to branch before finally falling to the ground. Billi batted the bird to and fro between his paws for a good five or six minutes, giving it plenty of time to escape, and when it didn't, he gobbled it up. Then he sat by the riverbank for a peaceful hour or two, watching the sun set while waiting for a fish. One appeared just as the last rays of the sun disappeared, and Billi snared it. Greedily, he dined on his second course, licked his whiskers, and started for home. He could hear sounds of music and laughter coming from the human villages he passed, but he refused to be tempted, not even to sneak a quick peak. He was very full. He needed a rest.

On the second day of Diwali, Billi catnapped in his cave for hours. But late in the afternoon, he broke down and headed for the villages. He didn't want to miss the festivities altogether, after all. He wanted to see the two-foots dressed in their new holiday clothes, worn in honor of Lord Krishna's victory over Narakasura, a legendary tyrant, and the bright village decorations. Doorsteps would be adorned with *rangolis,* the intricate red chalk designs, and windowsills would be flickering with oil lamps, lit to show Rama the way home from his exile. People would be passing around sweets or fish, and maybe, if Billi was lucky, one or two morsels would fall unnoticed to the ground, for him to sample later, after the humans had gone to bed.

Billi padded down his usual path, past the cave

where he had been born, a grove of silk cotton trees, and the bend of the river. He was nearing his favorite mango orchard when he saw a crack of lightning, followed by thunder. The sky was thick with churning black clouds, and the air was so oppressive that he could barely breathe. The monsoons were arriving.

One or two fat raindrops landed on Billi's nose, and then, with no other warning, a deluge began. Billi leapt up into a mango tree for cover, but within seconds he was drenched. Sheets of water were pouring from the heavens, the winds were howling as if pursued by evil itself, lightning and thunder were cracking apart the sky. Billi covered his eyes with his paws and moaned. It was the end of the world, he knew it.

The tumult went on and on. Suddenly, the branch that Billi was sitting on gave way. And before he could decide whether to stay put or jump, it crashed—into water. The whole orchard was floating. The river had overflowed its banks and was roaring through the forest, carrying trees and everything else in its wake.

Billi dug his claws into the branch with all his strength. To fall into the churning, rapidly moving water could spell his end. He had to stay on the branch.

Through his fear, Billi could hear the faint cries of humans caught up in the same terrific flood. Some were floating by him and screaming for help, others were going under. He saw a small girl child *whoosh*ing past rapidly, flailing to keep afloat. It looked like the girl he'd seen at the orchard! Other humans and a large dog were floating nearby on a piece of broken roof and screaming, "Nandini, Nandini!" But they could do nothing to save her. She was going under. At that moment, the dog leapt off the roof and swam rapidly toward her. The girl grabbed his fur and held on tight.

Then, as suddenly as it had started, the storm stopped. The river retreated. The flood was over. Billi crawled out of the water and collapsed, vaguely aware of Nandini and the dog lying safely on shore farther upstream. He fell asleep.

When Billi awoke some hours later, he found himself to be within three tree lengths of a house. Built on a small hill, it had survived the flood intact. Billi dragged himself toward it, hoping to find Nandini and the dog inside. He was curious—perhaps concerned—to see if they were all right.

After leaping gracefully onto the window ledge, he peered in through the window. Inside, he saw dozens of humans crowded around a roaring fire. Many were wrapped in blankets and appeared to be in shock. Lying in a place of honor, curled up directly in front of the fire, were Nandini and the dog. She had her arms around him, and he had his paws around her.

Involuntarily, Billi let out a sharp "m'-*roww*"—he was so happy that they were safe, he was so unhappy to be damp and bedraggled outside that cozy scene, and alone. No one had ever cuddled him like that.

Suddenly, a mass of two-foots came swarming toward him.

"Get away, you horrid *billi*!"

"You filthy beast!"

"He's looking for meat! He wants victims of the flood!"

"Kill him! Kill him!"

Pots and plates came hurling toward him, and some of the men were grabbing sticks and spears. Terrified,

Billi bounded away into the forest and darted up a tree as fast as he could. He crashed from branch to branch, tree to tree, hollow to hollow, hill to hill. He had to get away, away, away from those horrible humans. How he hated them.

Billi spent the several months of the monsoon season in his cave, moping, venturing out only briefly to hunt when the rains let up. As was usual during the storms, he had nothing to do, no one to talk to, no one to play with. Instead he thought and thought, occasionally batting at an imaginary speck of dust floating through the damp darkness. Did he really want to return to his beloved mango orchard, so close to humankind, after the rain subsided? Shouldn't he ignore humans altogether from here on out? That's what other cats did. And really, that last encounter with them was unforgivable. Imagine those two-foots thinking that he was after the kill when all he wanted was to see whether Nandini and the dog were all right.

On the other hand, Billi still felt strangely drawn toward the upright creatures. As his mother had said so many years ago, it was as if there were some sort of unfinished business between their two species. But what could it be?

Billi didn't want to become a pet, of that much he was certain. To be at another species' beck and call, like that dog? Unthinkable. He would die first.

And yet . . . Was it really his destiny to remain forever apart from all other creatures? Did he really have no choice in the matter? Why did he have to be like all other cats? Cats were extremely individualistic—everyone knew that—why couldn't he carve out his own way to be?

The two-foots would probably laugh if they knew that Billi was pondering such things, he thought. They seemed to assume that wild cats had no feelings. Talk about a failure of the imagination. Why should solitary creatures have fewer feelings than sociable ones?

Which brought up another point. How could Billi even think of trying to befriend a species that was so out of touch with the animal world? Humans seemed to know nothing about cats. Even worse, they didn't seem to *want* to know anything.

Throughout the monsoon months, Billi puzzled and

pondered, pondered and puzzled, catnapped and slept. Outside, the rains poured, the lightning flashed, the thunder cracked. And then he had it! When the monsoons passed, he would make a trip across south India, talk to as many animals as he could about the two-foots, and listen closely to what they had to say.

The day the rains finally stopped, Billi woke up and stretched, a very long, sensuous stretch, arching his back and reaching out with his front paws. He padded outside, blinking at the dewy sunshine, and dragged a few brambles in front of his cave, paid a final visit to the mango orchard, and set off on his quest. Now that the sun was shining again, the whole world seemed to be rejoicing. The forest seemed lighter, the sky bluer, the fields greener, and the clouds whiter than Billi remembered them ever being before. He ran, he leapt, he glided, he dove. Up one tree, down another, through a meadow, and past a cove. How lucky he was to be alive!

Billi galloped past all his favorite haunts and then slowed down. He had reached a part of the forest that he'd never explored before and didn't know exactly where to go. Not that it mattered. He trusted his instinct. He would find his way. He always did.

Rounding a corner, Billi heard a faint rustling noise and suddenly saw a huge and powerful cat racing toward him, claws extended, in full hunting mode. This is it! Billi thought as the yellow blur whipped toward his head. My life is over.

But it wasn't over. The yellow blur was passing and Billi was still standing. Human shouts were coming from somewhere nearby, along with the hisses of arrows and spears. Somehow, Billi had landed in the middle of something he had witnessed once before: a tame cheetah hunt—that bizarre ritual in which humans used a captive cheetah to help them track, corner, and kill their prey.

The movement stopped. He looked around for the cheetah, who, amazingly enough, was standing obediently off to one side, quietly studying the poor, panting antelope that he had cornered. Five of the hunters were heading toward the doomed beast, while a sixth strode over to the cheetah and tied a black hood over his head. Billi felt shocked at the sight, but he was torn: half wishing that the man would put a hood over his head, too, and give him earplugs. He couldn't bring himself to look at the antelope.

Gingerly, Billi approached his cat cousin—who appeared to be a very hungry cheetah, after all—and introduced himself. Much to his surprise, the cheetah was amiable and willing to talk, though it was a bit difficult to hear him through his hood.

"I don't really understand what's going on," Billi said. "Why are you hunting for these men? Do you love them so much that you want to help them kill? Do they love you?"

"Not at all," the cheetah said. "These men keep me hooded all day, even when I'm in my cage. That's hardly a sign of love—on either side. No, I'm afraid these humans admire me only for my ability to hunt. Apart from that, they're completely ignorant of my nature. They think, for example, that I'm a solitary creature. Female cheetahs are solitary, it's true, but we males are not. We band together and hunt together."

"I didn't know that," Billi said. "Is that why you can be tamed?"

"In a way. We're used to company, and we enjoy

company. But we certainly don't engage with humans out of our own free will."

"You don't?"

"Of course not."

"But I thought men caught you as babies and trained you to hunt."

"Don't be ridiculous. Humans can't teach cheetahs to hunt. We have to be caught as adults, when we already *know* how to hunt. And then they force us to work for them."

"Do you get anything in return?"

"Not really."

"But aren't you fed and protected?"

"From what? We have very few enemies in nature. And we know how to feed ourselves, thank you very much."

"But you enjoy the hunt, don't you?"

"Sure, but only because we're doing what comes naturally."

"Why not escape?"

"Believe me, I think about that each and every time I'm let out. So does every other captive cheetah."

"So what's stopping you?"

"They keep me hooded all the time, for one thing, which disorients me. They remove my hood only when it's time for me to hunt. They don't want me to get my bearings on my surroundings."

"But still . . . couldn't you just run away when they do take off the hood?"

"Yes, but it's dangerous. They would try to recapture me—or even kill me. They have the mistaken idea that an escaped cheetah will return as a man-killer, out of vengeance. But vengeance is a human concept. We cheetahs neither forgive nor forget, nor seek revenge. We believe in prudence above all. To survive is all. You know that."

"What would happen if you refused to hunt? Wouldn't they let you go then?"

"No, I would be killed. Believe it or not, they would think me ungrateful."

In the background, Billi could hear the gurgle of blood. The men had cut the antelope's throat.

"So, if you were me," he said to the cheetah, trembling, "you would keep well away from two-foots?"

"Why, are you considering becoming a 'pet'?" The cheetah spoke in an odd, mocking tone.

"No, I'd die first! I'm just curious."

"Well, we cheetahs certainly want nothing to do with humans. But every animal is different, and each must judge according to his own needs and desires. Some animals get along quite well with humans. Or so I've been told."

"What about . . ." Billi hesitated, embarrassed.

"What?"

He forced himself to continue. "Do you think I could join a pack of male cheetahs for a while? See how I like it? I'm tired of being alone all the time."

The cheetah was silent, and Billi yawned, as if he didn't care what the cheetah was thinking.

"That's not a good idea," the cheetah finally said.

"Why not?"

"You're too small and weak, for one thing."

"And for another?"

"They might eat you."

Billi continued on his travels until he came to a small Buddhist village, which reminded him of ahimsa, the religious doctrine of harming no living being, animal or human. The Sanskrit scholar had once read a famous verse from the *Dasabhumikastura*. It told of a Buddhist monk, Kshemendra, who wrote: "I cannot endure the pain even of an ant." Nice sentiment, Billi always thought whenever he remembered that line, but what's his attitude toward us bigger animals? Saying and doing were two completely different things, especially among humans.

Take, for example, the Buddhist golden rule to do no harm. Pair it with the admonition that Buddhists should eat whatever was given to them. Did that then mean that Buddhists could eat meat if it was offered to them? Yes, apparently, because Buddhism did allow its practitioners to eat meat if they believed that the animals had not been killed on their behalf. Talk about sophistry! Billi thought. What did it matter for whom the animal had been killed? Dead was dead. If nobody ate meat, no animals would be killed. Every time someone passed up meat, lives were saved, period. To pretend otherwise was simply a way for humans to assuage their guilt.

On the other hand, surely it was a good sign of the potential of humans that Buddhists at least thought about animals and said that they didn't want to harm them. A superficial sentiment was better than no sentiment at all. And consider Emperor Ashoka, who after converting to Buddhism in 261 BCE erected stone pillars all over India proclaiming his good intentions toward animals. The most famous of these inscriptions read: "Formerly, in the kitchen of the Beloved of the gods, King Priyadarsin [Emperor Ashoka], many hundred thousands of animals were killed every day for the sake of curry. But now when this Dharma-rescript is written, only three animals are being killed [every day] for the sake of curry, namely two peacocks and one deer, and the deer not always. Even these three animals shall not be killed in the future.* "

That directive may have been only a pious wish on the part of a new convert that was never enforced, but what an extraordinary gesture! You had to love Emperor Ashoka for that.

Skirting the edge of the Buddhist village, careful not to alarm its yellow-robed monks and other human inhabitants, Billi kept his eye out for animals. But it was the

---

* "Rock Edict I," as translated in *Ashoka's Edicts* by Amulychandra Sen: Calcutta, Institute of Indology, 1956, p. 64.

middle of a very hot and humid afternoon, and everyone seemed to be asleep. Billi slipped inside the Buddhist temple for a moment, just to take a quick look. All around him were intricate sculptures and painted panels depicting the life and teachings of the Buddha. To one side was what looked to be the tomb of a holy man, covered with a marble dome on which was carved what Billi believed to be the Buddhists' wheel of life. How beautiful everything was! He wanted to take his time, study things carefully, take a sniff or two, but he didn't dare. He could hear the whispers of approaching footsteps.

Back outside and feeling thirsty, Billi made his way down to a nearby river. He bent to take a drink with his paws, as all good leopards do, when suddenly someone nearly pushed him into the water. A herd of water buffaloes was arriving, shoving against everyone and everything as they made their way into the river.

"Hey, watch your manners!" Billi shouted. Unlike some cats, he enjoyed the water—most Asian leopard cats did—but these bumptious beasts had no right to almost push him in!

A dozen placid, docile water buffaloes eyed Billi balefully but didn't say a word as they submerged their hot, lumbering bodies in the cooling stream. Was this docility a consequence of living happily beside humans? Billi wondered. Could constant contact with two-foots bring about such contentment and peace? And if so, was that bad or good?

Billi approached one of the giant beasts and offered him the soft trill of "Hello, I'm here."

The water buffalo grunted.

"What can you tell me about your life among humans?" Billi asked him.

Water bubbles were hugging the beast's gigantic jaw, and his eyelids were half-closed. "It seems to me we give far more than we get," he mumbled.

"You mean you work hard all day, only to be rewarded with sleep at night?"

The water buffalo grunted again. "If only it were that simple. Of course, your description is accurate, but I wasn't even referring to physical labor. I was thinking more about other things."

"How so?"

"Take our behavior toward our young. In the wild,

we are very protective of them. Males and females form tight circles around their calves so that no animal—not even your fierce cousins the tigers—can harm them. Our horns are formidable weapons, and when aroused, we are large and dangerous animals."

"What's this got to do with humans?"

"Patience, *billi*! Once, we protected a boy who was tending us from a huge, man-eating tiger. The boy was no more than twelve years old, and we all felt much affection for him. He was thin and gawky, with long, spindly legs. He reminded us of our own calves. The tiger came out of nowhere—as sudden as lightning—but just as quickly, we circled the boy and lowered our horns. The tiger prowled and prowled, growling and snarling, but we wouldn't budge, and finally the nasty beast slouched away."

"Was the boy grateful?"

"Who knows? That's precisely my point! He must have been, but he certainly didn't show it. He told everyone in the village what had happened, and everybody thought it was marvelous, but did that translate into any kind of affection for us? No, of course not! We got no special treats! We continued to work just as

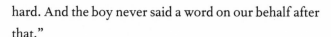

hard. And the boy never said a word on our behalf after that."

"Would you protect him again, if he was in danger again?"

"Without a doubt."

Billi put one paw in the water. He was considering going in. "Maybe humans just don't like water buffaloes," he said. "Maybe they're prejudiced."

"Naw, it's not that complicated. Two-foots simply don't give us that much thought. All they ever notice about us is that we're strong. That's true, of course, but I would like to be known for something more than just a physical attribute! And the humans admire our strength only because they're so weak themselves. That says more about them than it does about us. It's an odd thing, really—animals that humans know from mythology are important to them. But except for the cow, animals that they see every day—like us, or chickens or geese—are more or less invisible. None of the tales of the former lives of the Buddha, for example, ever mentions the water buffalo."

Billi tried to remember if he'd seen any water buffalo depicted on the walls of the Buddhist temple. He didn't think he had, but then, he'd been inside for only a few minutes.

"What about your milk?" Billi asked. "I've heard that your milk is richer and more satisfying than cow's milk, and that people in India drink more of it than cow's milk. Don't humans appreciate you for that?"

"You're right about our milk. But again, since unlike the cow we don't figure in religion, we're invisible to humans as *beings*, animals with an inner life, with preferences, needs, desires. That's why, to tell you the truth, I really wasn't all that surprised when that boy and the villagers weren't more grateful to us for rescuing him. All they said was, 'Those beasts acted out of instinct.' Humans always say that about animals when we do something they don't understand."

Billi was silent for a moment, trying to sort out what he had just heard. "But isn't it a bit odd," he said at last, "that you still feel affection for this species that doesn't love you back?"

"You have a good point," said

the water buffalo. "I've often wondered about that my-self. But I still haven't found an answer. It's just one of life's mysteries, I guess."

"And what about . . ."

"What?"

"Well, I don't mean to be rude, but I've heard it said that humans in India consider water buffalo unclean and don't allow them near holy places."

"Alas, that's true."

There was an awkward silence, and Billi saw a deep sadness welling up in the water buffalo's eyes.

"We don't know why that is," the water buffalo said. "We've always been a good friend to humans—plowing their fields, pulling their carts—even though they overwork us and beat us and even murder us in cold blood. They still sacrifice us, you know. They think it'll bring them favor from their gods. It's a repulsive ritual—especially since they try to make it all okay by apologizing to us before killing us. How absurd!"

"They're superstitious," Billi said.

The water buffalo didn't answer.

"What you say makes me loathe them even more," Billi said, "but for some mysterious reason I feel a strange pull toward the two-legs. Do you think I'm crazy?"

The water buffalo dunked his nose in the water. "Well, to tell you the sad, pathetic truth," he said, coming up, water dripping, "we're still hoping our relationship with humans will improve. They are capable of learning, you know, and we're still optimistic. Maybe one of these days they'll see us for who we really are."

"I wonder . . . ," Billi said, slipping into the water next to the buffalo. "Could I stay here with you and your herd for a while? I'm tired of living alone, and you and I have much more in common than I'd realized. I'd never even talked to a water buffalo before today, and I think if I stayed with you, I could learn a lot about friendship."

"I'm flattered," the water buffalo said. "*We're* flattered. It would be great fun to have a mascot for a while. But the trouble is . . . well, I really don't think you'd fit in. You couldn't help us plow or pull carts. And the humans wouldn't want you here. Our friendship would scare them. Humans are scared of everything they don't understand."

Billi wandered on. How complicated this business

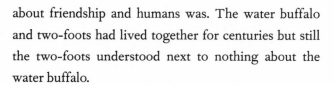

about friendship and humans was. The water buffalo and two-foots had lived together for centuries but still the two-foots understood next to nothing about the water buffalo.

Continuing along the river, Billi came to the outskirts of what seemed to be a large and wealthy Hindu village. He could see the towering, pyramidal roof of a Hindu temple, built of complex decorative layers, one placed on top of the next. Just the thing! He would seek out a cow. As a creature revered by the Hindus, the cow would undoubtedly have some very interesting insights into human nature. And if any animal had a good relationship with two-foots, it would be the cow.

But first Billi made a stop at the Hindu temple. He had already seen a Buddhist temple, and he wanted to compare the two. The Sanskrit scholar had made him curious about many things.

After waiting until the entranceway was empty, Billi padded inside, to find himself in a passageway crowded with images of Hindu gods. He recognized Vishnu, the god of the cosmic order, whom the scholar had called a redeemer of humanity. Vishnu looked like a human with four arms, each one holding something different: a lotus, a conch shell, a discus, and a mace. Beyond Vishnu was his consort, Lakshmi, the goddess of wealth; his son Murugan, the protector; and the chubby, elephant-headed Ganesh.

The scholar had had many fascinating things to say about Ganesh. He had called him the remover of obstacles and the patron of learning. Ganesh was said to have used the broken tusk in his hand to write down parts of the *Mahabharata*—the same text that had told of the hypocritical, religious cat. Ganesh had originally had a humanlike head, but the god Shiva lopped it off after Ganesh, guarding the goddess Parvati's door, refused to let Shiva in to see her while she bathed. Filled with remorse at what he had done, Shiva then sent out servants to bring back the head of the first creature they found. That creature was an elephant. Ganesh was restored to life and rewarded for his courage as a guard by also being made the lord of new beginnings.

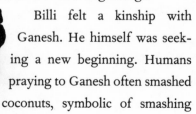

Billi felt a kinship with Ganesh. He himself was seeking a new beginning. Humans praying to Ganesh often smashed coconuts, symbolic of smashing

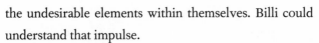
the undesirable elements within themselves. Billi could understand that impulse.

Billi wanted to venture more deeply into the temple, but he didn't dare. He was worried that once inside, he might become trapped, unable to find his way out. And he could all too easily imagine humans chasing him down dark corridors, silver knives flashing.

Carefully avoiding the bustling village marketplace near the temple, Billi next found his way to a rickety barn. He slipped inside. Dusk was falling and the barn was dark, but Billi could see perfectly—even better, in fact, than he could in bright sunshine. He noticed a milk bucket near the door and stopped to lap up the leftover creamy white liquid inside. He hadn't realized how hungry he was.

"I suppose you think you can just come in here and rob me of my milk, just like the two-foots," a deep voice said.

Billi looked up to see a large, almost fat, female cow staring at him, her round eyes hard as glass.

Billi averted his gaze. To stare another animal directly in the eye was to express hostility, and he wanted to make it clear that his intentions were friendly.

"I'm sorry," he said. "I didn't think. I was hungry, and the milk was just sitting here. I guess I should've asked first."

"You guessed right." The cow looked down at him over the side of the stall. "The two-foots never ask, either. They simply assume our milk is theirs for the taking. But like every other mammal on this planet, we produce our milk for our young and our young alone. What in the name of Lord Krishna makes you cats and humans think you can simply come in here and take and take without giving anything back?"

Angrily, she flicked her tail back and forth, dislodging the hundreds of flies that called her rump home.

"But the humans do give something back," Billi said, watching the flies as they resettled. "After all, the Hindus treat you as if you were gods. They worship you, glorify you, deify you."

"Oh, great. That and five rupees will get you a chapati."

"But you appear in many of their greatest myths. You are referred to as the earth herself, and as the mother of the gods. You are the ultimate symbol of the Female. What an honor."

"Honor my foot! How little you know. All that's more theory than practice. Why, look at the way the humans take our calves away from us just after birth, when every mother knows that there's no greater sorrow than to be deprived of one's child."

"They take your calves away?" This was the first Billi had heard of the practice. "Why?"

"Why do you think? So they can get more milk, of course!"

"Oh." Billi blinked at the cow, trying to show his sympathy. "Maybe the humans don't realize how much you miss your calves?"

"Nonsense. You're being naive. All they have to do is listen to us moaning."

"But what about the doctrine of ahimsa—harmlessness toward all beings? Doesn't that help protect you?"

"Maybe some, but we've suffered our share of exploitation and death, believe you me. Humans always do what's most profitable or convenient for them. They never think about others."

"Well, at least the orthodox Vaishnavas, the followers of Lord Krishna, are strict vegetarians. They may take your milk, but they don't take your life."

"Agreed."

"And don't the Vaishnavas call the highest heaven Goloka, 'the World of Cows'? That must make you proud."

"Why? Who cares? Heaven, paradise . . . these are abstract notions. What matters is the here and now."

"You must know the legend of how the baby Krishna protected his entire village of cow herders from a fierce storm by lifting up a mountain and using it as an umbrella?"

"Yes, of course." The cow's eyes softened. "It's a pretty image. And the mountain, by the way, was called Govardhana, which is another reference to cows. It means 'cow prosperity.' But you know, even though we cows appear in many Hindu myths, the humans aren't thinking about *real* cows. They're making religious points about human values. They're much more interested in themselves and their own salvation than they are in cows."

Billi thought of the classical Sanskrit texts about the hypocritical cat on the banks of the Ganges. This had been true of that story as well, of course.

"Still, it seems to me," Billi said, "that cows are better off than most animals in India. After all, you can't be killed or harmed—at least most of the time—and you're free to wander the streets as you please."

"Actually, you're wrong there. Most of the free animals you see are bulls. Haven't you noticed the three vertical white stripes painted on their foreheads? That's the *trishul,* which means they're sacred to Shiva and can roam unmolested. But unmolested does not mean taken care of—"

"Wait a minute," Billi said. "Three white stripes?" The Sanskrit scholar in the mango orchard had had three stripes painted on his forehead, too.

"Don't tell me you haven't seen those? Where have you been? The stripes are symbolic of Shiva's trident, which is in turn representative of the Trimurti—the Hindu triad of Brahma, Shiva, and Vishnu. Shiva is the lord of death and destruction and the lord of growth and rebirth."

"How can he be both?"

"How can there be birth without death?"

"I'm not sure, but—"

"I'm not here to give you religious instruction! I want to get back to your misconception about cows wandering happily about the streets. Haven't you ever taken a good look at them? Do they look happy and well fed to you? No, quite the contrary! Most have been let loose—or rather, abandoned—because they no longer give much milk. They're utterly neglected. Many are also sick and receive absolutely no care."

"What about the *goshalas*—cow hospitals? Old cows can go there, right, if they need help?"

"Another misconception. How many *goshalas* have you seen? There aren't nearly enough. To me the whole gesture rings a bit hollow."

"At least it's a gesture in the right direction."

"Yes, of course. But my point is that for all the noise the two-foots are always making about how much they love and honor us cows, they do precious little to put their money where their mouth is."

"Have you let them know how you feel?"

"We let them know all the time!"

"I find that hard to believe," Billi said. "It seems to me that cows aren't very good at expressing emotion. One time I saw a group of cows standing around another sick cow and staring at it without uttering a sound. No one made any attempt to help her."

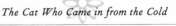
"You missed the entire point. What do you think was going on there? Yes, we cows don't have the physical capacity to do much. But that doesn't mean we don't feel. Those cows were offering the sick cow their silent moral support. Their presence was soothing and healing to her."

"Oh," Billi said. "Sorry. I didn't realize."

"Tell me the last time you saw a cow killed by another cow. It's never happened. Humans certainly can't say as much."

"If you could change things," Billi said, "would you stop associating with humans?"

"Definitely. Right now, we're living a kind of hell on earth."

"And yet I would have thought that you of all animals, deified by the Hindus, immortalized in human mythology . . ."

"As I told you, things aren't exactly as they seem."

"Right," Billi said, edging toward the door. "I guess they never are."

He said a quick good-bye. He had to get away. Being with the cow was profoundly depressing, much more so than being with the cheetah and water buffalo.

Why was that? he wondered. The cow's situation was much better than that of those two animals. She wasn't locked in a cage all day with a hood over her head; she didn't have to plow the fields and haul carts from dawn to dusk. But everything about the cow was black and bitter. Her advantages hadn't helped her at all.

Billi spent the next few weeks indulging in his senses. The whole forest seemed to be in bloom, and he spent hours wandering from orchid to orchid, poppy to poppy, jasmine to jasmine. Each individual flower had its own shape and scent, and they bewitched him with their splashes of bright color and intense perfumes. Especially delicious were the white and blue lotus. Each blue lotus had what looked like a little gold throne inside, and one day Billi tasted one. It was scrumptious. He'd found his favorite new dessert.

The silk cotton trees were in bloom, bursting with yellow, as were the flame-of-the-forest trees, bursting

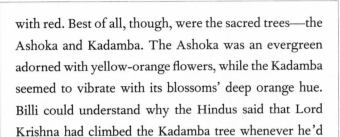

with red. Best of all, though, were the sacred trees—the Ashoka and Kadamba. The Ashoka was an evergreen adorned with yellow-orange flowers, while the Kadamba seemed to vibrate with its blossoms' deep orange hue. Billi could understand why the Hindus said that Lord Krishna had climbed the Kadamba tree whenever he'd wanted to hide the orange clothes of his *gopis*.

Billi passed plenty of wild animals, too. Troops of pale-faced bonnet macaque monkeys, watching him with alert eyes as they scrabbled over nuts and berries. Hordes of lion-tailed macaque monkeys, thick manes of gray hair growing from their cheeks and temples. Herds of four-horned antelope, Indian gazelles, and blackbucks, leaping away as soon as they sniffed his cat scent. Wolves hunting in packs. Indian foxes chasing after rodents. A sloth bear, calmly pulling honey out of a hive with its short front legs. Billi even thought he saw his cousin the tiger one day, too, but he couldn't be sure. The shy creature slipped out of sight too quickly.

One morning, wandering peaceably along as usual, Billi heard a wave of crashing sounds approaching. The crashes were so loud and rhythmic that they could mean only one thing—an elephant hunt. Humans were at it once again, this time chasing an elephant in the hopes of capturing him. Billi ran as fast as he could as far as he could in the opposite direction from the noise. He couldn't bear to watch.

To be of any use to the humans, Billi knew, an elephant had to be at least twenty years old. Much younger than that and its legs would not be strong enough to perform the feats of strength that humans required of him—pulling up trees, moving giant logs, carrying huge litters with half a dozen two-foots inside. The elephants were kept chained even while they worked, and at night it got worse: they were chained back and front, so they could barely move. No wonder elephants rarely slept—though that was also true in the wild.

The "taming" process of the captured elephants was unspeakably cruel. The elephants were starved, mistreated, and beaten in a ferocious battle to extinguish their will to fight. No wonder female elephants kept in captivity never gave birth. They didn't want to bring children into such a world. Humans should take note of that and learn something, Billi thought.

But what Billi really couldn't understand was why the already captured male elephants joined in the hunt-

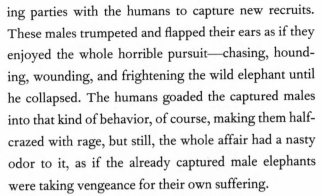

ing parties with the humans to capture new recruits. These males trumpeted and flapped their ears as if they enjoyed the whole horrible pursuit—chasing, hounding, wounding, and frightening the wild elephant until he collapsed. The humans goaded the captured males into that kind of behavior, of course, making them half-crazed with rage, but still, the whole affair had a nasty odor to it, as if the already captured male elephants were taking vengeance for their own suffering.

Billi much preferred female elephants, although to be truthful, he knew only one. Yet what an extraordinary creature she was! Billi had come across her one day, standing outside a village, a two-year-old girl at her feet. Drawn into the earth around the girl and elephant was a circle, and every time the girl stepped outside the circle, the elephant reached out her trunk and gently pulled her back in.

"What's going on here?" Billi exclaimed in surprised delight. "I've never seen anything quite like this before!"

"I'm baby-sitting," the elephant said matter-of-factly. "The mother is busy with her other children and asked me to do her this favor."

"You're amazing!" Billi said. "I hope you're appreciated."

The elephant didn't answer, which Billi took to be a "no." The word *slave* popped into his mind.

But if the adult humans failed to show the female elephant proper appreciation, the little girl herself certainly did. She was showering the elephant with affection. She loved it when the elephant swept her up in her trunk and put her back, squealing, in the circle. She hugged the elephant's trunk as if it were a huge arm and kissed it again and again.

"My elephant friend," the little girl kept saying.

"My girl child friend," the elephant said back.

Billi felt a stab of jealousy. Why don't I do anything for anybody? he wondered. Why doesn't anyone do anything for me?

"There's something I've always wondered about," Billi said to the elephant. "I hope you don't mind if I bring it up. It's a bit rude."

The elephant just looked at him. She was very old—at least fifty, Billi thought—and he suspected that she'd heard it all before.

"Late at night," he said, "I sometimes hear what

sounds like the screams of young elephants coming from deep inside the forest. Could that be right?"

The elephant sighed deeply, her wrinkled gray body rising and falling, big as a tent. "Those are the screams of orphan elephants," she said. "Their mothers were killed in a hunt. They're having nightmares."

Billi didn't know what to say.

"Elephants are very sensitive creatures," the elephant went on. "We've been known to die of heartache, you know."

"Yes, I have heard that," Billi said.

"Humans say we're just 'sulking.' They can't seem to understand that we experience real grief. They have a saying: 'The dog may bark, but the elephant moves on.' But why do two-foots think they are the only creatures on earth to grieve?"

"I don't know," Billi said. He remembered how he'd felt when his mother left and when the Sanskrit scholar disappeared. He hadn't been able to believe that either one of them was truly gone, and he'd returned to the cave and the mango orchard again and again, restless, yowling mournful, long, loud calls, expecting them to appear at any minute.

"The two-foot has yet to be born who understands the souls of animals," the elephant said.

Billi continued on, heading as far south as he could go, to the region of Thiruvananthapuram on the very tip of south India. Tiny towns filled with red-tiled roofs and lush flower gardens dotted the hillsides, in between sprawling tea plantations and shady coconut groves. Billi rejoiced in the strange new landscape. He played hide-and-seek with his shadow in the plantations, jumped up on the foreign roofs, his head held high, sniffing the cool breezes with their tales of exotic flowers and trees. He climbed up to the top of one coconut tree after another, just to compare their views.

One day, on an especially tall tree, he met a coconut crab, hard at work sawing down a coconut with his giant pincer. The crab was half the size of Billi and, thus, a formidable opponent. Still, he was no match for a cat. Billi waited until the coconut fell to the ground and the crab climbed down the tree. Then he pounced. The terrified crab scuttled away, leaving Billi alone with the tasty fruit, cracked open from the fall. Billi dined on its firm young meat, drank its pure nutritious water, and licked his whiskers.

Another day, playing hide-and-seek with his shadow on a tea plantation, Billi came across a mongoose who was doing the same. The two animals chased each other up and down the rows for what seemed like hours—one ahead at first, then the other—before collapsing under the shade of a flame-of-the-forest tree. They introduced themselves. The mongoose said that his human family called him Riki. He couldn't remember his original name; he'd been taken from his own family when he was just a baby.

"What a happy coincidence for me," Billi said. "I've heard that mongooses often live intimately with humans. And since your personality and my personality are somewhat alike, I wonder what you think. What's it like to live with two-foots? Would you recommend it?"

Much to Billi's surprise, Riki stiffened. He looked as if he'd taken offense, and for a moment, Billi was almost afraid he'd run away.

"I'm sorry," Riki said at last. "But I'm not the right animal to talk to about this."

"Why not? You live with humans, you're something like me."

"True. But I've lived through a terrible episode that's forever prejudiced me against humans. I don't think I'll ever recover."

"Why don't you tell me about it? Maybe you'll feel better and I'll learn something."

"I've already told this story many times, and retelling it never helps me. But if you insist. . . .

"I once had a close friend named Nakula, a tame mongoose who lived next door in what seemed like ideal circumstances. She was never caged, not even at night, and was free to come and go as she pleased. She and her family were on the most intimate terms, and she was especially friendly with the youngest children. She played with them all day long, almost as if she were their sibling, and when a new baby came along, Nakula was as proud and happy as if she had a new sister.

"I visited Nakula on the evening before the tragedy, and she told me with great excitement how the next day she was to be given a special honor. The family had to go out for a few hours in the afternoon and they were going to leave the new baby alone with Nakula. The baby would be asleep in her cot, and Nakula was to guard her with her life, as if she were her own child. She was very proud of the trust that'd been placed in her.

"Now, as you probably know, mongooses and cobras are famous enemies. So much so that, in the wild, they try to avoid each other. They both know how bloody things can get. The cobra has the advantage of his or her venom, but the mongoose has the advantage of his or her speed, and it is rare that a snake gets the better of a mongoose.

"What happened the next day still haunts me.

"After their outing, the family was returning to their house, the father in front, the children and mother behind. They were all eager to see their small baby again. As they neared the house, Nakula ran out to greet them, as she usually did, though today she was limping and moving very slowly. The children noticed this immediately and cried out, 'What's happened to Nakula?' As she got closer, they saw blood on her face and screamed, 'Nakula's been hurt!' But when the father saw the blood, he was seized with a horrific thought: Nakula has attacked our baby girl and killed her. Enraged and numb with grief, he yelled to the children to stand back, picked up the unsuspecting little Nakula, and hurled her against a tree, over and over, deaf to the pleas of his children and to the moans of the mongoose. He didn't stop until the little body lay limp at his feet.

"The children ran to Nakula while the father, trembling, ran into the house, to the baby's crib. And what did he find? A peacefully sleeping baby. Next to the crib lay the body of a giant king cobra, the most venomous of all snakes. Evidently, the cobra had approached the crib, only to be challenged by Nakula. The fight must have been furious, but the king cobra lay dead, covered in his own blood and that of the valiant Nakula.

"The father let out a wail such as I have never heard and fell to the ground, sobbing. He ran back to where the children sat with the dead body of their now lost friend and called her name over and over. But it was too late. . . ."

The mongoose sighed. "Why, I keep wondering, had the father assumed the worst about Nakula? Why hadn't he had faith in his friend? Why was he so easily swayed? After all, he'd trusted Nakula enough to leave the baby alone with her in the first place. Why the rush to judgment? Why couldn't he have been more like his children?"

"Children understand animals better than adults," Billi said.

"Yes, certainly, that's usually true."

"And women seem to understand better than men."

"That's often true, too," Riki agreed. "It could be their experience as mothers. They're used to watching out for other creatures."

The two new friends stood up and stretched. It was getting late. The sun was setting, splashing the sky with orange and pink.

"Would you like to come to my house?" Riki said suddenly.

"What do you mean?"

"Just what I said. The humans are away, visiting relatives. And you could meet Bana. He's a tame parrot and could give you another perspective on humans."

Ten minutes later, the two friends reached Riki's house and entered through a window that Riki had opened earlier. His human family liked to lock him in when they went away, he explained, but he knew how to unlock the latch and was always careful to lock it again after he'd returned.

Inside, the house smelled delicious. Spices were in the air: cloves, cinnamon, cardamom, cumin, chili—Billi thought he could smell them all.

"Yes, the women here are excellent cooks," Riki said. "They make killer *parathas* stuffed with potatoes, and *masala dosa*—have you had that? It's curried vegetables wrapped inside a pancake made of lentil flour. Or how about *idlis*? It's a rice dumpling served with lentils and chutney. The humans usually eat that for breakfast."

Billi shook his head. He'd never eaten much human food, except for a few rotis and garlic naan, which he hadn't cared for much.

"Here, have a taste." Riki pointed him toward a large bowl heaped with food.

"Wow, look at all that," Billi said.

"My family is very generous," Riki said. "They always leave treats out for me, especially when they go away. Try whatever you like."

Billi bit into a piece of spicy eggplant, followed by peas and cheese in gravy and a piece of deep-fried vegetable cake. Everything was delicious. It might be worth living with humans just to get food as tasty as this every day.

"What's that cat doing here?" someone said.

Nervously, Billi looked around but couldn't see anyone but Riki.

"Up here," a voice said, and Billi looked up to see a parrot perched on a wooden rod inside a cage hung from the ceiling.

"How did you get in there?" Billi said, horrified, before he could stop himself. Though he'd heard about it many times, he'd never actually seen an animal in a cage before. How small and dreary it looked!

"Don't ask," Riki said.

"I have a vague memory of a net descending on our flock one night while we were sleeping in a banyan tree," the parrot said in a monotone. "I wasn't much more than a baby at the time. My parents were with me, but that was the last time I ever saw them. Whether they died of fright in the struggle or managed to escape, I can't say. I was taken to a market and sold, along with everyone else."

"And you've lived in a cage ever since?"

"More or less. Though I do get let out for good behavior every once in a while. Usually just a few moments. Big deal."

"What about other parrots? Do you ever see them?"

"No, never, though I hear them sometimes, passing overhead. And when I do, I have a desperate longing to be part of a flock. I can feel it gnawing away inside of me, like hunger. Parrots were never meant to be alone."

How different from cats, thought Billi. Perhaps this explained some of the enmity between their two species? Better not to give voice to that thought.

"Is that why you speak with your human family?" Billi asked. "To have some sort of contact?"

"Please don't call them my family. My family is unknown to me. And I don't speak with humans, either. I chatter, I imitate. I do it for fun, to please them."

"So you *do* feel some affection for them?"

"Sure. Why not? I like being around them. They're an interesting enough distraction. Adjust or perish, you know. But it's really just a faute de mieux, isn't it?"

"You mean you'd rather be with a flock of parrots than a flock of humans?"

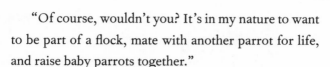

"Of course, wouldn't you? It's in my nature to want to be part of a flock, mate with another parrot for life, and raise baby parrots together."

Mate with another parrot for life. The phrase made Billi shiver.

"Why don't you just fly away, then, when they let you out?"

"Don't you think I would if I could? Here, look at this wing. The two-foots mutilated it so I can't fly away. I'm not even sure I should call myself a parrot anymore. How can I be a parrot if I can't fly?"

Billi didn't know what to say.

"Oh, the humans *mean* well enough," the parrot said impatiently, talking more to himself than to Billi as he walked up and down his cage, rocking it back and forth. "They feed me well and try to keep me healthy. They pick me up from time to time. They handle me. They talk to me. But that's just not good enough."

Billi was getting tired of traveling. He wanted to take a good long rest. But before he did, he wanted to visit a

Jain village. If there were any humans in the world who understood animals, he thought, it would be the Jains. Even more than Buddhism and Hinduism, their religion was centered on the concept of ahimsa, or nonviolence toward all living things. And the Jains believed in a very stringent form of ahimsa. Their monks carried brooms to sweep away any insect or worm they might inadvertently harm, and some wore face masks to avoid breathing in bugs. Jains filtered their water, so as to drink no organisms. They avoided eating vegetables that grew in the earth in order to do no harm to the animals clinging to the vegetables' roots. Farming was also forbidden to pious Jains, so they worked mostly as merchants, and very successful ones at that, since ahimsa also prohibited lying, meaning that the Jains were much trusted. Many Jain villages also contained a *pinjrapol*, which was a kind of hospital-cum-sanctuary for all types of animals—mostly cows and bullocks, but also goats, sheep, and sometimes cats, dogs, and pigeons.

One room in the *pinjrapol* was especially unusual: the *jivatkhan*, or insect room. Every morning, after the Jain women swept their homes, they would put their sweepings, including unharmed insects, outside their door. A man employed by the *pinjrapol* then made the rounds, shouting, "*Jivdaya!*" or "Compassion to the living!" and picked up the sweepings to take them to the insect room. There was even a rumor, probably apocryphal, that some extremely pious Jains occasionally offered their bodies to the insect room so that mosquitoes and other insects could feast on their blood.

The founder of the Jain religion, Mahavira, also known as Jina, the conqueror, had made one of the few human statements to which Billi could heartily agree: "All beings shun destruction and cling to life. They long to live. To all beings life is dear."

Many Jains lived in the Karnataka region, a land variegated enough to contain rice paddy fields and parched plains. Compared with Hindus and Buddhists, the Jains were few in number, but they had erected what was said to be the world's tallest monolithic statue—a seventeen-meter-high statue of Bahubali, a Jain saint. The statue was naked, and so, too—or so Billi had heard—were the most pious of Jain monks. Their nudity was a symbol of their renunciation of all worldly things.

The Bahubali statue stood atop a small rocky hill.

Human pilgrims left their shoes at the bottom and climbed barefoot up the hill's five hundred steps, hewn out of the rock face. Billi waited until the sun was setting, in order not to alarm the worshippers, and then bounded up the hillside to the high-walled courtyard in which the huge statue stood.

The Sanskrit scholar had once spoken about Bahubali. As the story went, Bahubali was the son of an emperor. When his father died, he and his elder brother fought fiercely over who had the right to the throne. Bahubali defeated his brother three times in successive contests, giving him the right to the emperor's title. But no sooner had Bahubali won the crown than he realized the futility of struggling and renounced his kingdom. Withdrawing from the material world, he entered the forest, where he meditated in complete stillness until he attained enlightenment.

Billi stared at the statue and wondered what it was thinking. Bahubali had a serene smile on his face. Vines were entwining his arms and legs, and anthills surrounded his feet. Snakes slithered between his toes, and birds were pecking at his shoulders. Had Bahubali understood the souls of animals after he reached enlightenment? Billi wondered. And if so, had he passed that knowledge on to other Jains?

Leaving the statue, Billi wandered down into a nearby village. Coming toward him was a pack of dogs.

Here are the very animals I need to speak with, Billi thought. These dogs live among humans and yet don't seem to be pets—that must be the influence of Jains. They still travel around in a pack; they are truer to their dog nature than that big brown dog I know from the mango orchard.

But as the dogs came closer, Billi realized that something was very wrong. The dogs looked horribly undernourished. He saw their bones moving under their skin and scabs on their haunches and bellies. Their fur was dull and matted. They didn't look as if they'd received any affection in a long, long time.

"Welcome, stranger," the dogs said to Billi.

"Thank you," Billi said, but he felt a bit nervous. The dogs looked very, very hungry.

"You're a pilgrim?" the dogs asked.

"In a way."

"Have you come from the Bahubali statue? Did you see any scraps of food along the way? Sometimes the two-foots leave stuff, after their picnics."

"I didn't notice," Billi said. "But why are you so thin and hungry? Doesn't anyone feed you?"

"Like who?"

"Two-foots."

"Never, although sometimes they let us eat from their garbage."

"And the sores on your body? Don't the humans look after them?"

"Are you nuts? They never touch us except to beat us."

"You're considered unclean?"

"Yes, because we eat garbage. But what else can we do? We don't have homes. And we're not wolves."

"You don't live with families?"

"We wish! No, very few dogs do, either in this village or in any other. Rare is the dog who can make that claim—one in a thousand, perhaps. Oh, sure, some of us once lived with families, or our mothers or grandmothers did. But either the families moved away, without taking us along, or they threw us out on the streets soon after we were born. Too many puppies, they said."

"What about the *pinjrapoles*? I thought they offered sanctuary to animals in need."

"Well, the *pinjrapoles* do have something called the *kuttakiroti* ritual—*rotis* for the pariah dogs. They feed us these from time to time. But the *rotis* aren't very nourishing, and there aren't very many of them. It's no more than a gesture, really, though it's not unappreciated, believe you me! Most non-Jain villages have no such tradition."

So the Jains don't do much for animals, either, Billi thought dejectedly. For all their talk of ahimsa, they sounded no better than the Buddhists and Hindus. Why did humans bother creating such beautiful and idealistic religious principles if they didn't follow them? What was the purpose of their splendid temples and statues if it was all a hoax?

"Aren't there any dogs in the village who live with humans?" Billi asked.

"Only one. His name is Shona. He lives just down that street."

Billi found Shona in a well-kept yard outside a well-kept house. He looked nothing like the dogs he'd just met. Shona's fur was shiny, his eyes bright and healthy. He looked content.

"What's it like living with humans?" Billi asked. "Do you recommend it?"

"Compared to what?" Shona asked in reply. "Some things are right and good. I like lying at the feet of the adults, playing with the children. They feed me. They brush me. I get taken on walks. But other things are not so right and good. I can't go outside whenever I want. I'm not free to investigate smells on my walks. At night, I'm locked in the house."

"So you never walk with the other dogs in the village?"

"Never! My family doesn't let me associate with them. 'Low-lifes,' they call them. But these dogs are my brothers, not 'pariahs.' I'd like to get to know them, hear their stories, learn about their lives."

Shona growled softly. "Oh, I know I should count my blessings. I'm know I'm lucky to live with a family.

They take good care of me. But I'm also a dog! I want to play with other dogs. Dog-play and human-play are completely different things. I want to chase other dogs, run with them, explore with them. I want to sniff other dogs, I want them to sniff me. I want to be with friends who are like me and who will immediately understand me without having everything explained."

"Do the humans understand you?"

"They understand the simple things. They know when I am happy or sad or even disappointed. But there are many other things that only other dogs can understand."

"What happens to you when your family leaves for the day? Are you left alone?"

"Very much so. My family thinks I don't mind, but I do. All dogs mind terribly. Our wild cousins the wolves are always together. And we dogs are descended from wolves. We are identical to wolves in many ways. Their experience is in our collective memory."

Billi had now spoken with many animals who had some close association with humans. And what he had learned gave him pause. He had not seen much evidence of understanding between humans and animals.

Why, then, was he still drawn to the two-foots? All in all, associating with them seemed a very risky undertaking. How could he hope to become the *only* animal to have a mutually satisfying relationship with humans? How could he hope to achieve what seemed to have evaded all the others? Especially since all the animals he had spoken with belonged to sociable species, preselected, as it were, to be with humans, another sociable species. He alone came from a completely solitary species. No animal from a nonsocial species had ever been domesticated. As a male Asian leopard cat, he had evolved to be completely by himself except for brief encounters with females. There was nothing in the cat experience to warrant optimism.

And looking at it from another angle, why would two-foots want to associate with cats? Humans seemed to want to live with animals who were useful to them: the cow gave milk, the elephant provided labor, the cheetah hunted, the water buffalo plowed. Only the parrot and a few lucky dogs seemed exempt from any assigned tasks. But the parrots and dogs were treated more like toys than living beings.

What, then, was Billi hoping for? What was in his mind? He was *meant* to be alone. Yet, nonetheless . . . He had a vision that wouldn't leave him alone. He wanted a richer and more complex life. He wanted some other being to know how he felt, and he wanted to know how that being felt in return.

But no other cat he knew of had ever chosen to throw in his or her lot with humans. Did he dare be the first? Did he dare ignore the wisdom of thousands of cats over thousands of years? Was he the only cat ever to experience loneliness? And if his forebears had experienced loneliness, and endured it, why couldn't he?

Over the past months, Billi had learned many things about humans that were distinctly unpleasant. He had learned that humans had little understanding, or desire to understand, who animals really were. He had learned that humans were guided largely by ignorance, prejudice, self-centeredness, and greed. He had learned that despite their idealistic-sounding religions, humans could be deeply hypocritical.

Billi thought to himself: I must not allow myself to

be deluded, to hope for something that cannot be. But I would like to try to subvert the process of domestication and to get humans to do what I, an animal, want, instead of the other way around. I would like to associate *with* two-foots, but I don't want to do anything *for* two-foots. I would like to have their companionship and friendship, but I must be allowed to come and go as I please. They must accept me as I am. They *must* not try to confine me. If they do let me be independent, I will reward them richly, with my friendship and love. But if they insist on confinement of any kind, I will plot my escape.

Almost nine months had passed since Billi had embarked on his travels, and he was tired. And homesick. He longed to return to his favorite mango orchard and to his cave. He longed to go birding and fishing in the Kerala backwaters. He wondered how the little girl, Nandini, and the big brown dog were doing. He wondered if the preparations for Diwali were beginning. It was almost that time. The threat of a new monsoon season was in the air.

Suddenly, Billi felt in a desperate hurry. The idea of

spending the holidays and the rainy season in an unfamiliar place was terrifying. He had to get home!

Billi raced through the hills and the valleys, the forests and the plains, making a straight line for the Kerala coast. He stopped only when absolutely necessary to catch a mouse or take a quick catnap. He was no longer interested in talking to other animals or in seeing new things. He had learned enough about the big wide world, at least for now.

Finally, Billi arrived in his mango orchard. It looked different. Some of the branches and trees were missing—that must be because of the flood. The orchard also seemed smaller—that must be because of his travels. He'd seen so much of the world now, including some exquisitely beautiful spots, like the rice paddies in the backwaters of Kerala or the hills near Ootie where there seemed an endless vista of mountains and forest for his sharp eyes to feast upon. Still, there was nothing quite as peaceful and cozy as the orchard. Billi climbed onto his favorite branch, stretched out in the sun, and fell asleep.

An hour or so later, he heard a familiar voice speaking familiar words.

"Hurry up, Nandini! Mother is waiting!"

Billi peered down to see Nandini, her brother, and the big brown dog approaching. They looked so well! The children had grown, and the dog was in his usual high spirits. How wonderful it was to see them again!

"I don't care," Nandini said. "Let's just sit for a moment. My foot hurts. I think I stepped on a thorn."

The children sat at the base of Billi's tree, and he watched as Nandini's brother examined her foot.

"There," he said, pulling out a thorn. "But you're all right, it didn't go too deep."

The big brown dog sniffed the air curiously and then looked up at Billi.

"You're back!" he yelped. "Where have you been all this time?"

The children looked up, too.

"There's a *billi*," Nandini said, but she didn't seem at all frightened, and neither did her brother. Billi forced himself to stay put.

"Come down, why don't you?" said the dog.

"Here, *billi, billi*," Nandini called softly, while her brother made a gentle whistling sound.

This is it, Billi thought. With his heart in his mouth, he descended the tree trunk and walked toward the children and dog. He was shivering. He'd never been so close to two-foots before.

"He seems so friendly," Nandini said. "He's almost tame."

"Don't bet on it," her brother said.

Billi stopped in his tracks. He would never be *tame*.

"Come here, *billi*, come here. Don't be afraid. We won't hurt you."

The sound of Nandini's voice was intoxicating. Billi started walking toward her again and then, before he was ready, felt the weight of her hand on his back. He startled. It felt so heavy. It felt so light.

"Your fur is so soft, you're so beautiful," Nandini said. She smoothed her hand over his pelt again and again, and to his surprise, Billi felt a deep rumble rising up out of his belly and lungs, vibrating through his entire body. He was purring! He hadn't purred since he had been with his mother.

"Listen to that sound he's making," the boy said.

"Isn't it wonderful!" Nandini said, her eyes shining. "Have you ever heard anything like it before?"

"Who are you?" the boy said to Billi, kneeling beside his sister. His touch was rougher than hers, but it still felt good. He started scratching Billi's neck, and Billi stretched back his head. What a delicious feeling!

"Hey, you kids, be careful! That's a wild cat!"

The children froze. Billi's legs stiffed, his back arched, his fur rose. An angry-looking man was approaching.

"Get away! Scat! Scat!"

Billi hissed. The dog barked.

"Get out of here!"

"No, don't," Nandini and her brother cried.

Suddenly the man lunged forward and Billi leapt back, into the forest, racing away as fast as he could. He didn't stop until he reached his cave, which looked exactly the same as when he'd left it. What had he been thinking? He couldn't be around humans. It wasn't safe. They were much too unpredictable. He thought forlornly of the purring sound he had been able to make for the first time since he was a kitten. Would he ever be able to make that sound again?

Two days later Billi was back in the orchard, watching out for more two-foots. He couldn't give up so easily. Not after all he had been through, and all his agonized thinking. Change took time. He couldn't expect miracles overnight.

With Diwali again approaching, the human traffic along the path abutting the orchard was heavy once more. Billi studied the people as they came and went, wishing he could stick his head inside their bundles. But where were Nandini and her brother and the dog?

He waited and waited, both that day and the next two days, but the children and the dog failed to reappear. Did the children regret petting him? Had the other humans warned them against him? Told them not to return to the orchard? Or—even worse—had their encounter together meant nothing to them? Had they already forgotten him?

Well, it wasn't as though Nandini and her brother were the only two-foots in the world. Billi would just have to try his experiment with someone else.

He waited until he saw a kindly-looking family with young children, a boy and two girls, approaching, and he slipped down from his tree, trying to look as unthreatening as possible. He held his tail straight in the air and walked with a gentle sway to his hips. The family stared at him in surprise and then hesitantly came closer, their curiosity aroused. They told him what a beautiful cat he was and how happy they were that he wasn't afraid of them. He rubbed against their legs, and soon one of them dared to lift him up. Billi offered no resistance and, moments later, found himself being carried to a large and beautiful home on a hill. He was set down with much ceremony. Word got out and people started arriving from all over the village to see the unique sight of a wild cat sitting quietly on an enclosed veranda.

The first night went well. Billi felt safe and comfortable. His belly was full. He was given his own cushion for a bed. He spent the next day exploring the house and its wonderful garden, filled with delicious smells. He ate a few of his favorite blue locust flowers. But that evening, as Billi was resting on the front porch and looking out over the garden to the forest beyond, the man of the house picked him up and said that Billi had to be locked into the house at night—and watched over carefully during the day as well. Such a beautiful and valuable animal could not be left alone lest he be stolen or change his mind and return to the forest, the man explained.

This was precisely what Billi had feared. But he would not be a prisoner! He pretended to play along with the man that night, but the minute the door was opened the next morning, he shot past the entire family as quickly as he could, practically flying into the forest. He would never return to that family. And they would never understand that it was their own behavior that had driven him away.

Perhaps the other animals were right, Billi thought. Perhaps humans weren't capable of seeing beyond themselves and would never allow other creatures to enjoy the same freedoms that they themselves possessed. Two-foots wanted only to contain, to capture, to enslave, and to dominate—for which, absurdly enough, they expected gratitude and love.

Lost in thought, Billi didn't realize that he had almost wandered out of the forest and into the outskirts of a village. Catching himself just in time, he was about to run up a nearby silk cotton tree when he noticed the big brown dog. What was he doing here? And why did he look so unhappy?

"Nandini is sick," the dog said when Billi approached him. "Very sick. She was bit by a cobra four days ago."

"Oh, no," Billi said. If only Riki had been there to protect her.

"Do you want to see her?"

The dog led him down a small alleyway to the doorway of a tiny home. Billi looked inside. Nandini was lying, pale and shivering, on a cot. Her parents were bending over her, and her brother was sitting nearby, his head sunk in grief.

No one noticed Billi. Slowly, he approached the cot. Nandini opened her eyes. Her gaze met his, and at that moment, Billi felt something that he had never felt before. He could imagine what it would be like to be this girl, to be so sick, to worry that you were dying. He also saw that when she looked at him, Nandini forgot her illness for a moment and lost herself in the beauty of a splendid wild cat—himself.

Nandini stretched out her arms. "It is the *billi, our billi*," she cried.

Her parents looked from her to him in astonishment.

She wanted to hold him in her arms, Billi thought.
He could not refuse her. Cautiously, he took a leap up
onto the bed. Nandini's parents were holding their
breath, but the broad smile on their daughter's face was
bringing tears to their eyes. Billi settled into the crook
of Nandini's arms and began to purr and purr, louder
than he had ever purred before. Purring had the power
to heal, his mother had once told him.

The purring did seem to be having a hypnotic effect.
Nandini closed her eyes, but her smile did not leave her
face. She held Billi loosely in her arms. He snuggled up
close to her body.

"He's been sent," Nandini's mother whispered.

No, Billi thought, I came of my own accord.

The mother and father, still crying, looked on
with amazement. It was the first time, ever, that a
wild cat had trusted his body to a human.

Billi fell asleep. He and Nandini slept side
by side for many hours. When they both
awoke, Billi was still purring, and Nandini
did not seem to be as sick as she'd been before. Her parents were convinced that they
were witnessing a miracle.

But things are never as simple as they should be. The father was a kindly but conventional man. He said to his wife, "Look, it's true that this cat seems to be curing our daughter. But still, he's a wild cat. There's no such thing as a domesticated cat. We can't trust him. He seems to like sleeping near Nandini, but what if he suddenly becomes savage in the middle of the night? What if he attacks her while she's asleep? We can't let him stay here."

The woman was astonished. "What makes you talk like that? There's no reason to believe this cat would endanger Nandini's life. On the contrary, he's helping her. You yourself said it was our good karma that brought him to our family. How can you change your mind so quickly?"

"I'm only worried about the safety of our child. I'm sorry, but we cannot let a wild animal stay in our house. It's too risky."

Nandini could not believe what her father was saying. "I know this cat loves me and will never harm me," she said weakly, struggling to sit up. "If you force him to leave, my heart will leave with him. I beg you not to do it."

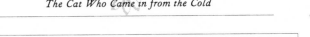

"I'm sorry, Nandini. Maybe one day you will forgive me. I have no choice."

"You do *so* have a choice, you just refuse to make it. You're a superstitious old man. I'll never trust you again." She buried her head in her pillow, sobbing.

From all the drama, Billi understood that he would not be permitted to stay. Sad but resigned, he made his way back to his cave.

But that evening, he was unable to settle down. I didn't even say good-bye to Nandini, he thought. It's not her fault that her father's so rigid. I must go back and let her know that I still care about her, that I didn't want to leave.

Although it was already dark, Billi made his way back to the house. And as he approached, he smelled smoke coming from the window near Nandini's cot. A candle had fallen over and the edges of her bedclothes were burning. The girl lay asleep, oblivious.

In a flash, Billi ran to her parents' bedroom, where the mother and father were just getting into bed. They looked startled to see him. He tugged at their clothes and made so much noise that they got up as he ran from the room. He ran back, then ran away again. Finally, they understood that he wanted them to follow him. He raced down the hall to Nandini's room. She was awake now and crying for help. The flames were nearing the bed, but she was still too weak to get up. The father doused the flames with water, and the mother rushed to her child. A few moments later, the fire was out.

Nandini looked at Billi with tears in her eyes. The mother and father looked at the girl with love and then at Billi with a similar expression.

"Yes, he is a wild cat, but he saved your life," the father said to Nandini. "And he seems attached to you. Maybe he is really somebody else, the reincarnation of an old friend."

What nonsense, Billi thought. But he couldn't blame the man. There was no precedent of a cat choosing to live with a human family.

Chastened, Nandini's father seemed to have undergone a major transformation in a single evening, in what the Buddhists called an *ashrayaparavrtti,* or "a revolution of the basis of one's existence." He was now ready to defy convention. He told Billi that he would be proud to have him live with his family and fought off the onslaught of disapproving neighbors who filed in over the next few days.

"Why are you letting a wild animal live in your house?" they cried. "How do you know you can trust it? It could attack you or your wife or your daughter at any time! Think about it, man—why do you think nobody has ever done this before? What makes you think you can get away with this crazy plan?"

"What you say is true," the father said, nodding, to all the objections. "But some things have happened that cannot be explained. I now know this cat will never harm us. On the contrary, he will be our friend, just like our dog. I feel it in my heart."

Then one day, to Billi's great surprise, the old Sanskrit scholar limped in. He had aged enormously since Billi had last seen him. His back was badly bent, and he could barely walk. So this is why he stopped visiting the orchard, Billi thought.

"Why, look who's here," the scholar said, slowly lowering his eyelids to blink at Billi. Billi blinked back. How did the scholar know that blinking was a cat's way of signaling affection?

"You know this cat?" the father said, astonished.

"I know his spirit," the scholar said. "And he's a very learned cat. He understands Sanskrit."

The father looked at the scholar as if he were crazy. "Since when does a cat understand Sanskrit? Or live with humans?"

"Who among us understands the way of animals?" the scholar answered. "They remain a mystery to us, even though we've all lived together on this earth for thousands of years. I have the feeling that this particular cat has had many, many lives. He may be older and wiser than us all."

"You book lovers are too much," the father said, half laughing and half grumbling. "You need to get a grip on reality."

The scholar just smiled. "You know," he said, "the world is constantly evolving. And something essential in the cat world may be changing. A strange thing happened to my daughter a few weeks ago—something similar to what's happening here. She was visited by a lovely female Asian leopard cat who seemed oddly friendly. The cat let my daughter pet her and then fell asleep on our front porch."

Billi pricked up his ears. A lovely female Asian leopard cat who was also interested in humans? His luck was definitely turning.

"You must come by and meet her sometime," the scholar said to Billi.

"Oh, now I really know you're nuts," the father said.

"One thing you must never do," the scholar said to the father, "is confine a cat in any way. Have you learned that yet? Cats are very independent and must be allowed to come and go as they please."

Billi jumped up into the scholar's lap. He had finally found his home.

"As if I had a choice," the father said. "Nandini has already laid down the law in that department. Before I know it, this cat will have more rights in this house than I have!"

A few days later, Billi visited the scholar and his daughter. They petted him for a while and then left him alone to stretch out on their sunny porch. He was just nestling his chin into that wonderful spot between his folded front paws when into the courtyard walked the most enchanting creature he had ever seen. She blinked. He blinked. They touched noses. They sniffed. Moria was her name.

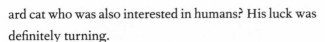

"What are you doing around humans?" Billi asked.

"I could ask you the same," Moria said.

"It's a long story."

"I have all the time in the world," she replied.

Moria still lived in the forest. She was not ready to live with humans. Never mind, thought Billi, she is mine. Together they climbed trees, walked the forest paths, went hunting in the mangroves. They talked all day. They talked all night. Never had Billi told anyone so much about himself. Never had he learned so much about another. He was falling in love.

Diwali arrived. On the first day of the festival, the humans scrubbed their houses and decorated their doorsteps with chalk designs. On the second day, they bathed themselves with oils before the sun rose and dressed in new clothes. On the third day, they worshipped Lakshmi, the goddess of wealth; on the fourth, they commemorated the visit of the friendly demon Bali; and on the fifth, men visited their sisters to have a *bindi,* or mark of devotion, put on their foreheads.

Billi and Moria shared in all the festivities. They listened to the singing and storytelling, they watched the dancing and gift giving, they dined on fancy breads and vegetable stews, and they ate endless, endless sweets. The only part of the festivities they didn't like was the firecrackers. The noise made them both flee into the forest, though Billi came back later, after he had calmed down Moria.

Watching the humans celebrate their religious festival, Billi had a glimmering of insight. *Religion helps humans dream of creating a more perfect world,* he thought. *Yes, many humans are deeply hypocritical, but perhaps one of these centuries they will learn to practice what they preach. Ahimsa may become reality yet.*

The monsoons came, and Billi watched the rains from the safety of his snug human home. Half of his day was spent on Nandini's bed, the other half in front of a roaring fire. In the evenings, he went out to visit Moria in her cave, and when the rains let up, they went hunting together. He had everything in life he had always wanted—security, love, independence.

But now Billi wanted something else, too, something he'd never wanted before. He wanted his own family. Yet unlike all the thousands of cat generations that had come before him, Billi also wanted to be part of his children's lives as they were growing up, to teach them what he knew. He wanted Moria to come live with him and the humans so that they could raise their family together there. He may have chosen to be the first cat to be domesticated, but he didn't want to be the last.

Moria listened to Billi. She thought how nice it would be to give birth to kittens in a place where others could help them and shelter them from danger. She also loved Billi and wanted to make him happy. She imagined the look on his face when their kittens were born. She moved into the house.

The humans were delighted. Moria was such a lovely Asian leopard cat. She was light brown where Billi was dark brown, slow and deliberate where he was fast and impulsive. Everyone came to love her, and soon she was sleeping with Billi in Nandini's bed. Three months later, she gave birth to eight kittens, the first ever to be born in a human home. A new era had dawned.

Billi and Moria taught their kittens to have no fear of humans, and the kittens purred as much for Nandini as they did for their parents. They played endlessly with visiting children. People from all over the village came to see the kittens and were immediately enchanted with the little fluff balls who seemed so adult even while they were so tiny. Everyone wanted a kitten, and Billi and Moria thought that when the time came, and the kittens were old enough, they would have a choice of many good homes to which to send forth their young, beginning what, from the cat's point of view, has become the *katiyuga*, the Age of the Cat.

And that is how, several thousand years ago, in India, the first cat chose domestication.

PHOTO: © CORINA KONING

JEFFREY MOUSSAIEFF MASSON, former Sanskrit scholar and project director of the Sigmund Freud Archives, has written more than twenty books, including *Slipping into Paradise*, *The Pig Who Sang to the Moon*, *The Nine Emotional Lives of Cats*, *Dogs Never Lie About Love*, and *When Elephants Weep*. A long-time resident of Berkeley, California, he now lives in New Zealand with his wife, two sons, six cats, and a menagerie of other animal companions.

ABOUT THE TYPE

This book is set in Fournier, a typeface named for Pierre Simon Fournier, the youngest son of a French printing family. Pierre Simon first studied watercolor painting, but became involved in type design through work that he did for his eldest brother. Starting with engraving woodblocks and large capitals, he later moved on to fonts of type. In 1736 he began his own foundry, and published the first version of his point system the following year. He made several important contributions in the field of type design; he cut and founded all the types himself, pioneered the concepts of the type family, and is said to have cut sixty thousand punches for 147 alphabets of his own design. He also created new printers' ornaments.

Pierre Simon Fournier is probably best remembered as the designer of St. Augustine Ordinaire, one of the early transitional faces. It served as the model for the Monotype transitional face, Fournier, which was released in 1925.